D1278372

Bellies to the Sky

A Bedtime Breathwork Book

By Colleen Canning

Illustrated by Allie Daigle

Beaver's Pond Press
Saint Paul, Minnesota

Bellies to the Sky: A Bedtime Breathwork Book © 2021 by Colleen Canning

All rights reserved. No part of this book may be reproduced in any form whatsoever, by photography or xerography or by any other means, by broadcast or transmission, by translation into any kind of language, nor by recording electronically or otherwise, without permission in writing from the author, except by a reviewer, who may quote brief passages in critical articles or reviews.

Illustrations, book design, and typesetting by Allie Daigle
Project Manager: Laurie Buss Herrmann

ISBN 13: 978-1-64343-786-6
Library of Congress Catalog Number: 2021901493
Printed in the United States of America
First Edition: 2021
25 24 23 22   5 4 3 2

Beaver's Pond Press
939 West Seventh Street
Saint Paul, MN 55102
(952) 829-8818
www.BeaversPondPress.com

To order, visit www.csquaredbooks.com.

Contact Colleen Canning at www.csquaredbooks.com for school visits, speaking engagements, and interviews.

To the love of my life — thank you for making me laugh every day.
I'm yours eternally.

—C.C.

To my mother, who endlessly encourages my personal and
creative growth.

—A.D.

It's time for sleep, little one, little one.

Now prepare for sleep.

Breathe in and raise your belly to the sky.

Breathe out

and let your belly fall to Mother Earth.

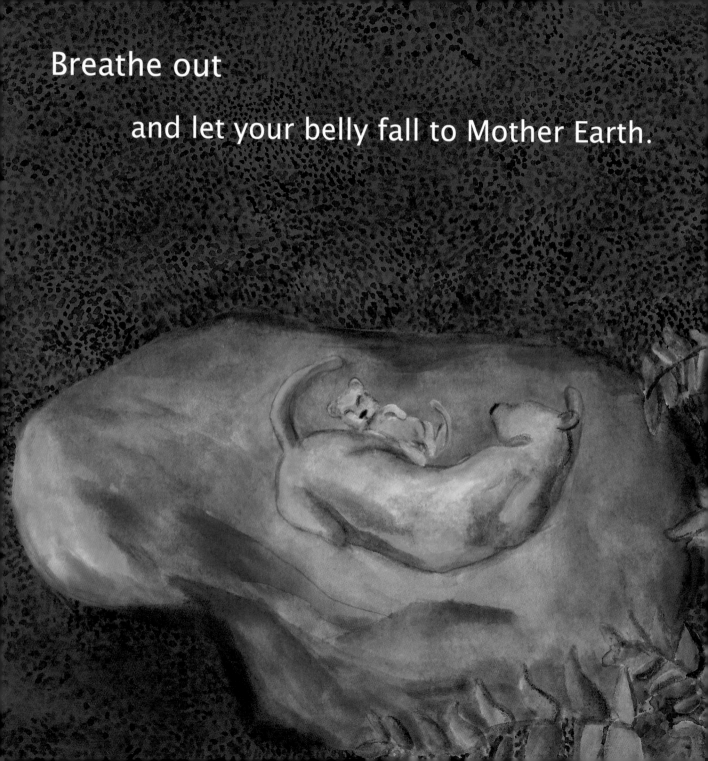

Breathe in...

Breathe out...

Now relax your feet
and relax your toes.

It's time for sleep, little one, little one.

Now prepare for sleep.

Breathe in and raise your belly to the sky.

Breathe out

and let your belly fall to Mother Earth.

Breathe in...

Breathe out...

Now relax your legs,
relax your hips,
and relax your belly.

It's time for sleep, little one, little one.
Now prepare for sleep.

Breathe in and raise your belly to the sky.

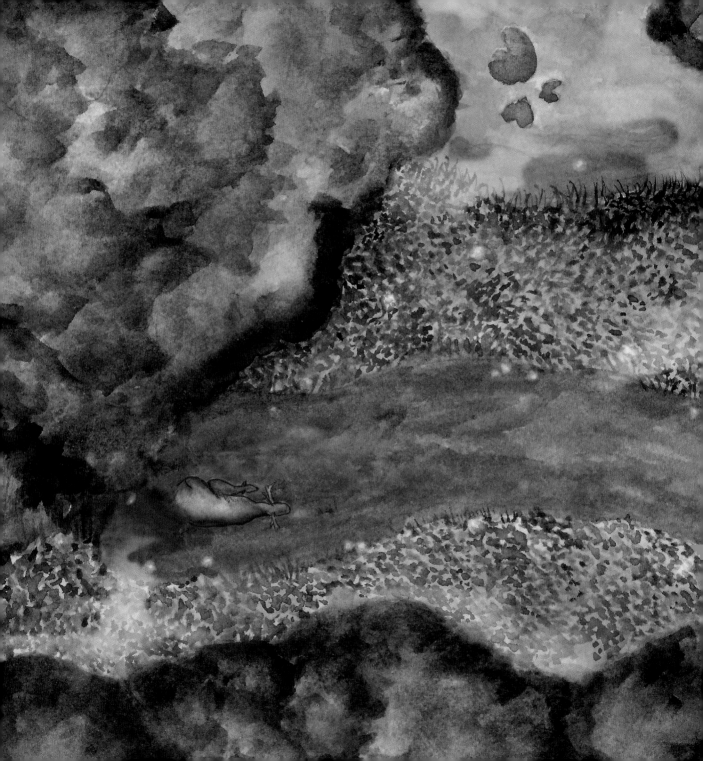

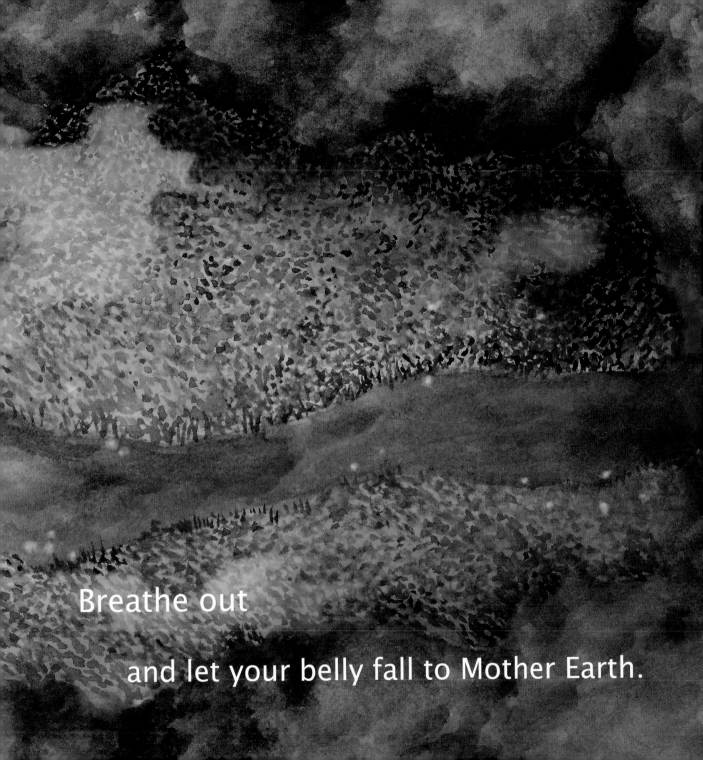

Breathe out
and let your belly fall to Mother Earth.

Breathe in...

Breathe out...

Now relax your shoulders,
relax your arms,
relax your hands and fingers.

It's time for sleep, little one, little one.

Now prepare for sleep.

Breathe in and raise your belly to the sky.

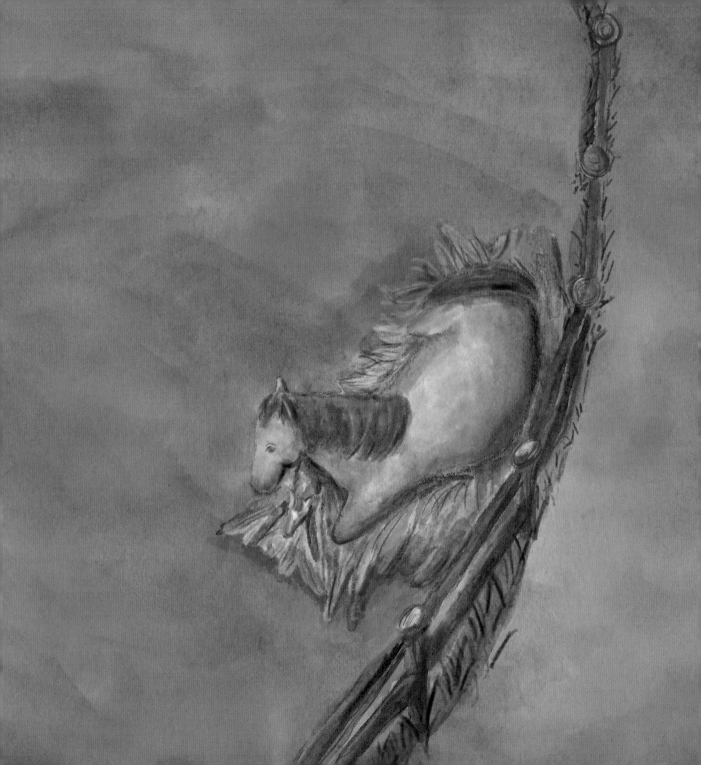

Breathe out

and let your belly fall to Mother Earth.

Breathe out...

Now relax your face,
relax your tongue,
and close your eyes.

Sleep now, my little one, little one.

We love you very much.

Our Animal Guides

(sometimes referred to as "spirit animals")

The animals in this book encourage us to breathe deeply to rest our minds and relax our bodies—starting with our toes and ending with our eyes—before sleep. With their help, our breath can fill us with a sense of calm and stillness. Do you have a favorite animal guide?

The Lion

symbolizes courage, strength, and a relentless spirit.

The Wolf

symbolizes intelligence, social awareness, and a strong instinct.

The Deer

symbolizes sensitivity, vigilance, and a gentle determination.

The Horse

symbolizes motivation, stamina, and a powerful spirit.

About the Author

Colleen Canning, her husband, and their dog, Loki, live in Minnesota and enjoy traveling around the world. They have four adult children, a son-in-law, and an amazing granddaughter. Colleen was a corporate executive and coach before shifting her focus to launch her first children's book, *Bellies to the Sky*. Over the past thirty years, she has experienced the benefits of yoga and breath teachings in India, Sri Lanka, Thailand, Malaysia, and the Bahamas. As a result, she felt inspired to create children's books that honor our imaginations and instill loving peace and stillness. Learn more at www.csquaredbooks.com.

About the Illustrator

Allie Daigle is an illustrator from Connecticut who strives to create detailed and immersive images that stimulate the imagination. Whether for a children's book, a product label, or her original pieces, Daigle's works implore the viewer to linger and explore the carefully crafted details within. Allie enjoys working as a freelance artist and is excited about her current and future creative endeavors. Outside of work, she loves taking trips and lazy downtime, preferably spent with friends, family, and her dog. See more of her work at www.alliedaigle.com.